GRADUATION HOCKEY WARS 15

SAM LAWRENCE & BEN JACKSON

Illustrations by Tanya Zeinalova

⚒ **Book # 15 - Hockey Wars Series** ⚒

www.indiepublishinggroup.com

Copyright © 2024 Sam Lawrence & Ben Jackson

ISBN: 978-1-988656-88-5 Paperback
ISBN: 978-1-988656-89-2 Hardcover

Editor: Mary Metcalfe

Promise me you'll remember:
You're braver than you believe,
stronger than you seem,
and smarter than you think.

——A.A. Milne, *Winnie-the-Pooh*

Other Books by Sam & Ben

Hockey Wars Series

Hockey Wars
Hockey Wars 2 - The New Girl
Hockey Wars 3 - The Tournament
Hockey Wars 4 - Championships
Hockey Wars 5 - Lacrosse Wars
Hockey Wars 6 - Middle School
Hockey Wars 7 - Winter Break
Hockey Wars 8 - Spring Break
Hockey Wars 9 - Summer Camp
Hockey Wars 10 - State Tryouts
Hockey Wars 11 - State Tournament
Hockey Wars 12 - Euro Tournament
Hockey Wars 13 - Great White North
Hockey Wars 14 - Class Trip
Hockey Wars 15 - Graduation

Softball Strikeout Series

Softball Strikeout - The New Girl

My Little Series

The Day My Fart Followed Me Home
The Day My Fart Followed Me To Hockey
The Day My Fart Followed Santa Up The Chimney
The Day My Fart Followed Me To Soccer
The Day My Fart Followed Me To The Dentist
The Day My Fart Followed Me To The Zoo
The Day My Fart Followed Me To Baseball
The Day My Fart Followed Me To The Hospital
It's Not Easy Being A Little Fart

If I Was A Caterpillar
Don't Fart in the Pool
Trevor Takes Flight
Ghosts Can't Play Hockey

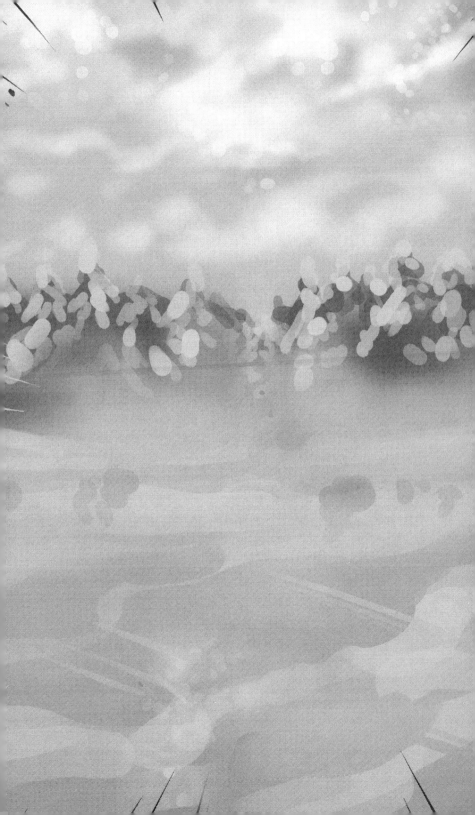

IT WAS ONLY two weeks until graduation, and the kids were driving their teachers around the bend.

As eighth grade drew to an end, the kids were all struggling to concentrate on their work, and unfortunately, the teachers were the ones left dealing with the consequences.

"Will this year never end?" Rhys asked, as the kids sat eating their lunches. "I mean, I feel like we've been here for years. I just want this to end so I can start high school."

"We have been here for years, Rhys," Georgia replied drily, "but I get it. It's hard to take it all seriously now that we're so close to leaving. At least we have the dance to look forward to. Won't you be sad when we leave middle school?"

"Yes, that's true, but—" Rhys began to say before being interrupted by Cameron.

"I asked Millie to go to the dance with me!" Cameron blurted out.

The conversation around the table completely stopped as everyone slowly looked from Cameron to Millie and then back to Cameron again, with looks of absolute disbelief plastered all over their faces.

"Just as friends," Cameron blurted out again, blushing, desperately looking at Millie to back him up. "We're just going as friends. To the dance, I mean. For graduation."

"Yes," Millie agreed, her face also burning red hot with all the attention she suddenly had focussed on her. "Cam asked me yesterday, and I said yes. It's no big deal."

Georgia raised one eyebrow, staring directly at Millie, but said nothing. Her look said it all, *'Girl, we need to talk.'* No words needed to be said between the two. Millie just nodded in agreement.

Rhys went to spin in his seat to look at his best friend and clumsily knocked his drink over, sending it flying across the table and causing chaos. Luckily for Cameron and Millie, it took all the attention off them and the announcement Cameron had just made.

Georgia took that opportunity to stand up, grab Millie by the arm, and lead her away from the

table into the corridor and under a stairwell. She needed to find somewhere to talk privately without the others listening in.

"First," Georgia began, as soon as Millie was safely away from the group, "why didn't you tell me? I think *'this little announcement'* was worthy of a text, if not a phone call. I want all the details. Spill the tea, please."

"Well, I was going to tell you today," Millie explained, "after lunch. I didn't think Cameron would randomly blurt it out at the lunch table in front of the whole group. We're just going to the graduation dance together as friends. It's not a big deal."

"There's no excuse for not telling me," Georgia said, rolling her eyes, "this is you and Cameron. Childhood friends. Romeo and Juliet. Destined to be together. It's a huge deal. Even if it's just *'as friends,'*" Georgia said as she made air quotes above her head.

"I'm not appreciating all the *'air quotes'* in this conversation," Millie said, mocking her friend. "Cameron and I can go to a dance as friends without it having to turn into anything else. We're not little kids."

"If you think that you're dreaming, and you're even more naïve than I thought you were," Georgia started to say before being interrupted by the bell. "We'll finish this later, Millie Anna Duncan."

4

Millie gulped. She knew she was in trouble when her best friend used her full name. "Okay."

The two friends rushed to class, slipping through the door and taking their seats several minutes later, earning them a glare from their English teacher for being late.

"We'll talk later," Millie whispered to Georgia.

"Okay," Georgia replied, "let's hope you don't kiss him by then and forget to tell me that also."

"Georgia and Millie," their teacher Mrs. Mae said from the front of the room, "first you were late, and now you're whispering. Is there something you'd both like to share with the class?"

"No, Mrs. Mae," the two girls chorused back, "sorry, Mrs. Mae. Won't happen again."

"Good," their teacher replied, "now open your books and turn to page 67. Georgia, you're reading first."

Georgia glared at Millie, silently blaming her for this, but quickly focussed on the page and began reading.

Later that day, after school had finished, Georgia and Millie were sitting in Millie's basement. The game controllers sat idly on the floor at their feet. The game was on the start page where it had been for over forty-five minutes since they first switched it on.

Neither of them really had any interest in playing. They both had other things on their minds.

"Two people can go to one dance as friends and still be friends at the end," Millie said, for about the tenth time. "I don't see why it needs to mean anything more than that."

"You're right," Georgia agreed, "two friends can go to a dance together as friends, and it would never turn into anything other than that. For example, I could go to the dance with Cameron as a friend and still be friends. Nothing would change. But, and this is a big 'but' Mills, you and Cameron aren't normal friends. You guys are so close to one another. You're basically boyfriend and girlfriend already."

Millie thought about what her best friend had said and then thought about it some more. Was she making a mistake? Was this whole idea a terrible mistake or the best decision she'd ever made?

"Now you have me worried," Millie said quietly, "Cam's my best friend. I can't lose him."

Both girls sat mute, each weighing up their response, before Georgia finally broke the silence.

"Mills, do you like Cameron?" she asked. "I don't mean like, I mean *Like* capital L like him."

Millie thought about it.

Then she thought about it some more before quietly answering, "Maybe. I don't know. This is a lot. There have been times when I thought I definitely had a crush on him. I was jealous that he got to spend all that time with Mia, but then I was with Liam, and I didn't think much about it. We love doing all the same things and hanging out together, but what if we took it to the next step, and it all went wrong, and I lost my best friend? Oh my gosh, what if Cam has a crush on me, or what if he doesn't?"

"Millie, calm down," Georgia said, hugging her friend. "You're spiraling out of control. Take a deep breath and relax. You don't have to make any life-changing decisions right now. Just relax."

"You're right," Millie agreed, "but I see your point. For now, let's just leave things as they are, and if anything changes between Cam and me, we'll go from there."

"Good idea," Georgia said, "now pick up your controller so I can kick your butt at this game again!"

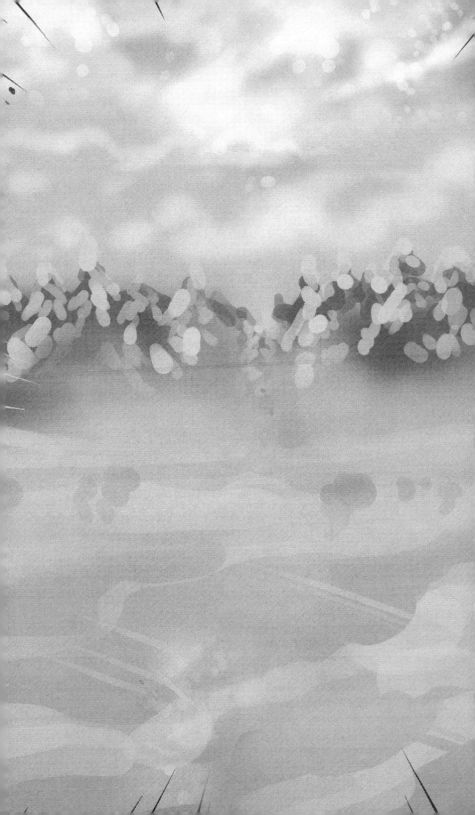

THE FOLLOWING DAY, Cameron waited outside Millie's house to walk to her school as usual. The two had been walking together to school since they were little, and now, it was a tradition. However, this morning, they were both unusually quiet, even awkward with each other.

"Cam—" Millie began to say, at the exact same time that Cameron said, "Millie—sorry, you go ahead."

"No, it's fine," Cameron said, "you go first."

The two friends hadn't spoken to each other since the incident in the cafeteria the day before.

Millie thought about what she would say, stopped dead in her tracks, and looked Cameron squarely in the eyes before starting, "I'm not sure what's in store for us in the future, but you're my best friend, and I can't lose you. Don't say anything.

SAM LAWRENCE & BEN JACKSON

I just need you to know this. I know we said we were only going to the dance as friends, but the whole thing has made me think about a lot of different scenarios, and I'm scared. I don't know how you feel or how you feel about me, but I just need you to know this."

"I feel the same, Millie," Cameron agreed. "I don't want to do anything that could possibly drive a wedge between us or our friendship."

"Okay, so we're both on the same page," Millie said, breathing a sigh of relief. Just knowing that she and Cameron felt the same way made her feel a whole lot better about the situation they both found themselves in.

"We're good, Mills," Cameron replied. "Neither of us will do anything to jeopardize our friendship. Well, now I feel better."

"Same," Millie said laughing, "I was just thinking the exact same thing. Lucky, it almost got weird there for a second."

"Right?" Cameron said laughing, "We're good."

The two of them relaxed, and the conversation started flowing naturally once again.

They switched to the secret party the parents planned for them after graduation. Or the not-so-secret party, as most of the kids knew all about it already but were all acting as if they had no clue what their parents were up to behind the scenes.

It wasn't long before the two kids turned the last corner, with the large iron school gates looming in the distance.

One day closer to graduation, Millie thought, *one day closer.*

The boys and girls of the Hurricanes and Lightning were both at the arena for an extra skills session. Their coaches had got together and booked a clinic for them, and by combining the two teams, they'd got a great deal.

"So, do any of you guys have anything cool planned for the summer?" Khloe asked as she sat strapping on her bulky goalie equipment. Because she wore the most equipment, she was often the first in the changeroom before a game and the last to leave after a game.

"Mom and Dad said they were thinking of getting a summer pass to the amusement park," Lola said, "as long as we use it a few times, it'll be worth it."

"It would be cool if we could all talk our parents into buying the summer park pass," Ashlyn agreed, "that way, whenever we wanted to hang out over the summer, we could do it at the park."

"Oh, that's so cool," Millie said, "and now that they have that shuttle bus back and forth from the

park, it would be super easy to get there, and our parents wouldn't even need to drive us every time."

"Aren't you going to the cabin again with Cameron, Millie?" Georgia asked sweetly, but the dramatic eye roll gave away what she was really thinking.

"I'm not sure," Millie said, ignoring her friend's sarcasm, "Mom and Dad haven't said anything about it yet, but most likely, yes."

In the changing room next to theirs, the boys were also having a conversation about their upcoming summer vacation plans, but theirs was a little different.

"Look, I'm just saying," Rhys lectured, "that summer is all about having fun, not making plans. The last thing we should be doing is planning activities."

"I get that, Rhys," Hunter said, agreeing with his friend, "but if we don't make at least some plans, it'll just turn into the usual scrambling around trying to get together while everyone is doing different things."

"I bet the girls are planning out their summer," Logan said, "they're always organized weeks in advance."

"I bet they are," Rhys said, rolling his eyes, "I just don't want to spend days planning out every minute of the summer break. What if I want to stay up all night playing games, and then I need to sleep in? Any plans that I'd made would be ruined."

"You sleep in every day," Cameron said laughing, "how would planning something to do on a certain day get in the way of that?"

"So funny," Rhys mouthed back dryly, "have you been taking comedy classes that I didn't know about, funny guy?"

"You guys about ready?" Coach John asked, sticking his head in the door, "or still busy gossiping?"

"On the way, Coach!" the boys all shouted back, throwing on the last of their equipment and heading out the door and onto the ice.

"That's it," the instructor, Gemma, shouted as the kids skated around the course she'd laid out on the ice, "smoother and cleaner through the corners. Smoother is faster, and faster is smoother! Let's go around again!"

The girls and boys were skating a twisty course around the arena, designed to teach them how to skate faster.

By skating smoother and cleaner, they wouldn't lose as much speed in the corners and could carry their speed longer out of the corners with less effort. It meant they'd be faster chasing down a puck while also using less energy, leaving them with more gas in the tank for later in the game.

Before this drill, the other instructor, Steve, had taken them through some puck-handling skills.

"Okay, great work," Steve said, "now let's combine the two drills. Grab a puck and skate the course again."

"Oh, and to make it a little more interesting," Gemma added laughing, "every time you lose the puck, you owe me starts and stops. One full lap for every time."

This announcement had a few of the kids groaning, but the two goalies, Logan and Khloe, just laughed, getting them glares from their teammates. They didn't have to do these speed skating drills, so they thought they would miss out on any punishment.

"Oh, you think that's funny?" Ryan, the third instructor, said. He'd been working with the two goalies off to the side while the other kids did their drills. "Don't worry. You're not missing out. In the next shooting drill, for every goal that goes into the net, you'll be doing a lap in full gear."

"Not so funny now, eh?" Rhys whispered under his breath before chuckling and skating away to join the rest of the kids lined up and waiting for their turn.

Despite their best efforts, plenty of pucks were dropped, and there were a lot of kids doing starts and stops at the end of the drill, but this only caused them to go into the next shooting drill with that much more thirst for success.

Seeing the two goalies and knowing what was on the line, all the kids shooting put in just a little more effort when they shot.

The two goalies also did their best, with Logan almost standing on his head to stop some shots, but inevitably, a few pucks still found their way into the back of the net, and the pair of goalies did the laps around the arena together, laughing and smiling, like they always did.

"How are those laps going?" Rhys chirped from the sideline. "About time we got you two out and about for a little tour of the whole rink. Can't have you just sitting in the net all day now, can we?"

"Laps are great, Rhys," Logan replied smiling. "I love a little exercise to get the blood flowing and the heart rate up. Great cardio, you know?"

"They're a great bunch of kids," Gemma said to Coach John and Coach Phil, who were standing on the sidelines watching and making notes. "I can tell they've been playing together for a long time."

"They are, and they have," Coach Phil replied. "Best groups of kids I've ever had the pleasure of coaching."

"Agreed," Coach John said, "even the boys, for the most part, are no trouble. They're getting a little more '*vocal*' these days, but overall, they've never argued or carried on at all. It's been fun coaching them and watching their skills evolve and change over the years."

Once they were done, the boys and girls split into mixed teams drawn randomly and had a quick pickup game before heading to the changing room.

It was the perfect way to end their training session and a good opportunity for them to release a little extra energy before heading home.

3

"I'M PRETTY SURE that plan's not going to work," Mia said, "so we should probably scratch that completely and work on some others."

"True," Millie agreed, "you're probably right. It was kind of silly."

Mia and Millie had been video-calling one another for a few hours, trying to devise a plan so Millie could finally visit Mia over the summer.

Mia had surprised Millie with a visit, but Millie really wanted to return the favor by visiting Mia, where she lived, and meeting her friends.

Currently, they were working on Plan F when they were interrupted by Millie's mom knocking on the bedroom door before walking in.

"Got any washing, Mills? Oh, hey Mia," Millie's mom said, waving once she realized that the two girls were video calling, "how's your mom and dad, Mia? Any plans for the summer?"

"Hey, Mrs. Duncan," Mia replied, "they're both great. Dad's super busy with his work as usual, but apart from that, all's going well."

"That's great, but what are you two up to?" Millie's mom said, looking suspiciously from one girl to another, "and don't think I didn't notice the giggling and whispering as I walked in. Spill the gossip."

"It's spill the tea, Mom," Millie said laughing, "not spill the gossip."

"Why would I want to spill tea?" her mom replied, shaking her head, "I don't even like tea. You know I drink coffee. You kids and your sayings. Anyway, what are your plans for the summer, Mia?"

"Oh, not much. You could say that I'm still in the planning stage. What about you guys?" Mia asked.

"We're going to the cabin with the Simonds again as per usual," Millie's mom started to say before Millie interrupted.

"Wait, we're going to the cabin again, Mom?" Millie asked, "You didn't tell me that. That's something I needed to know."

"We go every year, Mills," her mom said laughing and standing up to leave, "how about I tell you when we're not going? It'll probably be easier that way. So, moving forward, just assume we're going.

I'll let you know the date later so you can plan out your summer. Anyway, the washing won't do itself. I'll talk to you two later. Bye Mia, it was nice to see you, even if it was only on a screen!"

After the door closed, both girls burst into laughter, "I think she was sus," Mia said between giggles, "she knows more than we think she knows."

"There's not much she doesn't know," Millie replied laughing, "it's like living with a detective in the house, but if we plan it all out, I think we can make it happen."

"My parents are the same," Mia said, agreeing, "there's not much they don't know."

What Mia and Millie didn't know was that their parents were already a step ahead of them, several steps, in fact.

Both Millie and Georgia's parents had been talking with Mia's parents about arranging a trip so that the girls could hang out together.

Mia's dad would be in Dakota again in August for another training weekend, so they searched for some flights and found a cheap flight for both Georgia and Millie to fly back with Mia's dad and spend two weeks with Mia at her house.

As Millie's mom headed back downstairs toward the basement with the washing, she couldn't but smile as she passed Millie's room, thinking about the surprise she had planned and also how cute it was that the two of them were currently on the phone trying to come up with plans to see each other.

Spill the tea indeed, she thought, chuckling to herself. *These silly kids and their weird sayings.*

"Who do you think it will be?" Rhys asked the group of friends the next day during their morning break at school.

"Who do we think what will be?" Cameron replied, "what are you talking about, bro? You always start these random conversations like you've already had half the conversation in your head before you speak out loud."

"Valedictorian," Rhys answered, "who do you think it's gonna be?"

"Oh," Millie said, finally understanding what Rhys was talking about, "I don't know, but I don't think it's going to be me, that's for sure."

"You're doing heaps better with your grades, Mills," Georgia added, "so it could be. Your grades are better than mine now."

"No, they're not," Millie said smiling, "but thank you."

"I think they'll announce it after lunch," Khloe chimed in, "that way, whoever it is has time to pre-pare a speech and stuff for graduation."

"There's a few pretty smart kids in our grade," Hunter added, "but I think out of our group of friends, Ashlyn will be right in the mix to take it out."

Hearing her name mentioned, Ashlyn couldn't help but blush, "thanks, but I don't know. My grades are good, but there are some really smart kids in this grade who work really hard, too."

"You got it, sister," Daylyn said, hugging her twin, "I know it. And your grades are not good. They're amazing."

"Guess we'll find out soon!" Preston said smil-ing. "But either way, I'm hoping it's you, Ashlyn. You got this!"

"Good afternoon, kids," the principal announced, her voice cutting into the lesson via the speaker in their classroom. "Sorry for the interruption, but we have some exciting news to share before you head off to lunch."

Millie, Georgia, Cameron, and the rest of the group stopped and looked toward where Ashlyn sat quietly.

This was it, the valedictorian announcement they'd all been waiting to hear.

"I'm proud to announce that there were several very close contenders for this year's valedictorian award. For those of you who are not graduating this year, we're hoping to see the same high standards next year. But be warned, the standards set by this year's graduating class are extremely high, so you have some work ahead of you to top them. Anyway, enough from me. I know there are a few nervous kids waiting. This year's Valedictorian, and the student who has shown exemplary commitment to academic excellence—as well I might add to their sporting achievements—is . . ."

Ashlyn's heart skipped a beat. It was her. She knew it. None of the other kids potentially in the running for Valedictorian played any sports she could think of.

"Ashlyn Johnson, congratulations! You are this year's Valedictorian. Well done! Your hard work, commitment, and dedication to your academic pursuits sets a high bar for all our students. On behalf of the entire faculty and school, congratulations. Come up to my office between classes, and I'll go over the details with you."

All the kids jumped up and shouted congratulations, rushing over to hug Ashlyn and cheer her on winning the award.

Ashlyn was shaking hands and hugging, all while her face burned, so she looked like a tomato. She couldn't wait for the day to end so she could tell her mom and stepdad Phil that she'd won.

"This is so cool," Hunter said, giving Ashlyn a big hug, "not only are you a star on the ice, but you're also a whiz in the classroom."

"He's right," Khloe added, "we're all so proud of you. Well done, Ashlyn."

"Thanks, guys," Ashlyn said, for about the fiftieth time since the announcement.

By the time she'd been stopped by most of the teachers and half the kids in her grade on the way to lunch, her lunch break was almost finished, and she'd barely managed to take a bite of her sandwich.

"Now you get to do a speech at graduation in front of the whole school," Rhys grinned. "No pressure!"

"*Rhys!*" Millie shouted, punching him in the shoulder, "why'd you have to say it like that!"

"Oh, my bad," Rhys grinned even wider. "Never mind. I'm sure she'll be fine."

"I haven't even thought about the speech," Ashlyn groaned, rolling her eyes, and looking up at the sky as if someone would come to save her. "I have to give a speech in front of the whole school!"

"You'll be fine, Khloe. You got this, girlfriend."

"Thanks," Ashlyn replied, "I'm sure it'll be fine."

"Worst case," Rhys chimed in again, "just imagine that everyone's got no pants on. That always works for me when I have to give speeches or talk in front of the class."

"Have I told you you're a little strange, Rhys?" Khloe said. "Just a little bit."

"Hey girls," Ashlyn and Daylyn's mom said as the twins walked into the house after school, "how was school today?"

Ashlyn and Daylyn had devised a plan on the way home to trick their mom, and it was time to put that plan into action.

Nothing like teasing your mom to finish the day off the right way!

"Mom, you need to sit down," Daylyn said. "Ashlyn has something to tell you, and it's not good."

"What?" their mom blustered, "Ashlyn Johnson, what have you done? What's happened?"

"Well, I had to go and speak to the principal today. Mom, it's about graduation," Ashlyn explained, "I'm not sure you're going to be happy, but I feel like you need to know."

"Just promise you won't be mad," Daylyn added, "it's not her fault, Mom."

"Just tell me already! And if you're not graduating because you've gotten yourself into trouble, so help me," their mom said, butting in and spiraling just a little bit out of control now.

Of all the kids in the school, particularly her kids, she never thought it would be Ashlyn she'd be having this conversation with. She couldn't even remember when either of her kids had even been close to getting in trouble.

"I was named valedictorian, Mom," Ashlyn said smiling innocently.

"You were named valedictorian?" Janet asked, confused, "But. Wait. You were named Valedictorian! Why you little...you monsters! I thought you were in trouble. Oh my gosh, well done! And don't ever do that to me again. It's not nearly as funny as you think it is. I thought you were in some sort of trouble or something."

The three ladies jumped, hugged, and laughed until they cried, and then they laughed some more.

The girls' trick on their mom had been perfect, and it would be a while before they got her this good again, if they ever did.

"Well, let's go and celebrate. I think this deserves chocolate sundaes. What do you girls think?" Janet asked the twins.

"Sounds perfect, Mom," they both answered, "chocolate banana sundaes for dinner all round!"

FRIDAY FINALLY ROLLED around, and the group of friends managed to get organized, planning a trip to the movies. Despite the normal argument about what movie to watch, they eventually settled on one of the current superhero action movies doing the rounds.

"I'm just saying the book was totally different to this," Preston whispered across to Rhys, "like they could have just stuck to the original a bit more. Look at his costume. It's all wrong. The original had that red piece—"

"Shh," Georgia hissed at the two boys, "I didn't pay to come and listen to you two debate how real the movie is compared to the cartoon and what color their costumes are."

"Graphic novel, actually," Preston said, correcting her, "or comic book, but definitely not cartoon."

"We don't care!" Millie said hissing, "just watch the movie, eat your popcorn, and save the book club talking for after we're done, or I'll call that lady and have her come and kick the two of you out."

Preston and Rhys both rolled their eyes at the threat but stopped talking over the movie and instead switched to silently gesturing at each other, combined with a lot of eye-rolling for the next ten minutes.

Once the final credits rolled and the bonus scene played out—because you always need to stay for the bonus scene, which drops hints about the next movie in the series—the lights came on, and the debate between Rhys and Preston immediately kicked off again.

Not only did it immediately start again, but it continued all the way into the theater lobby.

"This is why I said we shouldn't do a comic book movie," Cameron said to Millie, "these two take it way too seriously. They'll be debating this for the rest of the night, if not tomorrow. Our group chat will be just these two talking about this movie."

"I know, right?" Millie agreed. "You're lucky you weren't sitting right next to them. I threatened to have them kicked out if they didn't stop talking."

"There's a reason I sat as far away as possible from those two," Cameron said laughing, "they've ruined enough movies for me in the past. I learned that mistake long ago with any movie that was created from a comic book."

"That was cool and all," Georgia said, "but I'm more looking forward to relaxing in your pool tomorrow, Preston. That's if we can keep the debating about books and movies to a minimum."

Saturday night was a pool day and BBQ at Preston's and everyone from both hockey teams had been invited, along with their parents. Swimming and a BBQ at Preston's was always one event you didn't want to miss, as his parents had a fantastic pool and hot tub and always cooked a feast of the best BBQ food.

"Of course," Preston said, "and sorry. I just take comic books pretty seriously, and I don't like it when directors don't stay true to the original stories and history of the books just to make some movies more appealing to the masses. You know what I mean?"

"I don't," Georgia replied, "I just like watching movies without running commentary."

"He gets right into it," Sage, Preston's girlfriend, said, "doesn't he? And if you get him started again, we'll be standing here in the lobby for another half hour. So, let's leave it for another time."

"Sorry," Preston replied, "comic book nerd. Guilty."

"It's okay," Sage said, hugging him, "it's one of the reasons I think you're so cute."

The group of kids hung out in the lobby for the next half hour, playing a few arcade games and relaxing until their parents showed up to collect them, and it was time to head home for the night.

It was a beautiful afternoon, and there was a highly competitive game of volleyball happening in the pool and the parents had moved their chairs closer to the pool to get in on the action.

Some parents had even been jumping in and out of the pool to lend a cheeky hand when the team they were supporting was short a player, needed a hand, or just wanted to throw a spanner into the works for their own amusement.

"Dad!" Cameron shouted, "You're in. I want to go and get something to eat."

"All right, bud," Cameron's dad replied, "kids prepare to get schooled in the finer points of pool volleyball. I hope that you have brought your notebooks. You're going to want to write this down!"

"We all use computers or tablets now," Rhys responded sarcastically, "not notebooks like they used to use when you two rode dinosaurs to school."

"Please," Millie's dad replied, "we used to walk fifty miles to school in the snow with newspaper wrapped around our feet instead of shoes. I think we can handle a few kids in a pool, buddy."

"Oh, here we go," Rhys shot back. "I was wondering how long it would take to bring up your epic journeys to and from school each day. Let's go. You can serve first."

Millie and Cameron were sitting together by the BBQ while they ate, watching the entire exchange between their dads and friends unfold in front of them.

"Your dad's hilarious," Millie said, taking another bite of hotdog, "he and Dad are totally teaming up and picking on the rest of them."

"I know," Cameron said laughing, "like they're not two fully grown men that are at least a foot taller than everyone else. Plus, they're twice as wide. It hardly seems fair, but everyone's having fun, and that's the main thing."

"The only good thing is that they'll run out of energy way before the rest of the kids," Millie pointed out, "so we'll be able to kick their butts soon enough."

"What do you reckon. Time to give these kids a school lesson they'll never forget!" Millie's dad said laughing, "before we retire for another cold beverage."

"Couldn't agree more, mate," Cameron's dad said, "let's do it!"

The following week at school crawled by for most of the kids. There was nothing like waiting for the end of the school year to make a few weeks feel like a few months!

However, it was a final opportunity to turn in any extra credit assignments they'd been working on and tidy up any outstanding assignments or projects. But, for most of them, it was just time to relax and enjoy the final days of school together.

It was the last whole week of school before they would graduate. For most of the kids, it was an exciting time but also a time of reflection and nervousness about what their future would bring next year.

5

"I THOUGHT TODAY would never end," Cameron said to Millie as they walked home from school on Friday afternoon.

"I know, right?" Millie agreed, "the whole week has dragged by, but at least now we only have one week left, and it'll all be over and done with."

No sooner had the words left her mouth than the idea of them finally finishing middle school and all the changes that would bring with it as they went off to high school started to loom in her mind.

"Are you okay, Millie?" Cameron asked, noticing how quiet she'd just gotten.

"Yeah," Millie replied, "it's just starting to sink in, I guess. These are the last few times you and I will walk home from school together."

"This school, Mills," Cameron said, reassuring her. "It's not going to be the last time we walk home together."

"I know, but our new school isn't just up the road. We'll probably be bussing most days," Millie said, "especially in the winter."

"Not going to lie," Cameron said laughing, "I could do without the walking to school during winter."

Millie laughed, "Don't like having wet socks and shoes all day?"

"Right? That's the worst!"

"Yeah, but if you wore the right shoes, instead of your 'cool guy' shoes," Millie air quoted, "you wouldn't have wet socks and gross feet. My shoes are toasty and dry all day."

"Yeah, yeah. Whatever!" Cameron said, rolling his eyes. "Oh, I just remembered. Mom said that you guys are coming over for a BBQ tonight. Is that right, or did I totally imagine that conversation?"

"That's right! I forgot about that. I'm hanging out with Georgia tomorrow," Millie answered.

"Cool, Rhys and some of the other guys and I are doing something with our dads tomorrow, golf or something," Cameron said.

"Golf or mini golf? Millie asked.

"Golf," Cameron answered, "you know, walk around all day hitting golf balls. That golf."

"What? You've never played golf in your life!" Millie said incredulously. "It's a little bit harder than just walking around hitting a ball."

"I've hit a few balls around," Cameron said, "but seriously, how hard could it be? I'm a natural athlete, after all. There isn't a sport I can't play."

"Natural athlete, my foot! But I guess we'll see, won't we? At least the girls and I are doing something fun. We're doing a spa and beauty day on Sunday."

"Ooh, fancy. Anyway, I'll see you later tonight," Cameron said as the two arrived at Millie's house, "I have a bunch of chores to get done before I come over."

"See you later!" Millie replied, "Have fun!"

"How was the BBQ last night?" Rhys asked, as he and some of the other boys stood around waiting for their dads to get everything organized at the golf clubhouse.

"Good," Cameron replied, "nice BBQ food, a movie, and just chilling—"

"That's nice," Preston said, interrupting, "and I would love to sit and chit-chat about BBQs all day, but it's time to get serious, gentlemen. Who here has played golf before?"

All the boys raised their hands. What they lacked in actual golf experience, they more than made up for in confidence. Some might argue there was too much talk and not enough action, but they were willing to give anything a go.

Rhys side-eyed Cameron, "He's taking this pretty seriously, huh?" he whispered.

"Yes I am, Rhys," Preston relied, "but let's try this again. I mean, who has, on multiple occasions, come to a golf course and hit golf balls around the course and successfully completed the course?" Preston asked, "for real."

All the hands went down except for Hunter and Rhys.

Cameron and Logan looked at each other sheepishly and just shrugged.

"That's better," Preston said, addressing the team of misfits assembled in front of him, "at least I know what I'm working with. Rhys and Hunter, how many rounds have you played?"

"I play a couple times each summer with Dad," Rhys said, "I'm only average, but still way better than Cam."

"Whatever, dude," Cameron said, rolling his eyes.

"I probably go out every other weekend," Hunter answered, "and I've had a few lessons. I'm not too bad."

"Okay, not bad. We're playing a format called '*the best ball*,' so we only count the best shot from the entire team. This way, it won't matter so much if someone has a bad round because we take the best shot from the group rather than the collective score. It'll be good for Cameron and Logan anyway. It'll let you learn a little without as much pressure."

"You boys all ready to learn a little golf lesson today?" Cameron's dad said as he approached, "we might not be able to outskate you, but I think we've got you beat on the golf course. You're about to get schooled in golf as we schooled you in pool volleyball the other day."

"Oh, here we go again," Rhys answered, "everyone prepare yourself for the epic '*in our day, we walked 750 miles through the ice just to get milk for breakfast*' story."

"And that was just one way," Preston's dad shot back, "and you don't want to know what we had to if we wanted to hang out with our friends. You kids these days..."

"Have it so easy," Hunter said, finishing the sentence for him, "and we'll never understand how hard it was back in the day. Don't worry. We get it."

"Anyway, I think it's time to let the golf skills do the talking. I know all of you dads spend every other weekend out here, but I think we'll be able to give you a good run for your money," Preston said, "should we begin?"

"Of course," his dad replied, "let's get this golf lesson started."

"We'll see," Preston said, "we'll see!"

"You said golf, right?" Georgia asked Millie as the two girls sat going through Millie's stuff, "you sure they didn't mean mini golf?"

"No, real golf. Apparently, they have a golf day, then dinner, and a few of the boys are having a sleepover at Cam's house after," Millie replied, "but yeah, I was confused about the golf, too. Cameron tried to tell me he's some sort of *'natural athlete'* or something, but I've never seen him hit a golf ball in his entire life."

"I know Preston and Hunter play every now and again, and Rhys has mentioned it before, but the rest," Georgia shrugged, "who knows? Cameron thinks he's awesome at every sport."

"True," Millie said, "he definitely doesn't lack any confidence."

Millie was doing a total cleanout of her room, and to keep her company, Georgia had come over to help out or look through all her stuff. Either way, Millie appreciated the company.

"Mills! Look at this," Georgia shouted, "it's the list from when we were battling it out with the boys! Why you kept this, I'll never know."

"I didn't know that I did," Millie said, laughing and looking at the list of names, "how crazy was it that we were all literally fighting over who got to play hockey on the pond."

"You didn't talk to Cameron for, like, a whole year," Georgia replied, "and now you're practically dating. Probably be engaged and married before you know it."

"Stop it. We are not dating," Millie said, rolling her eyes and throwing a pair of socks at her friend, "don't start that stuff already."

"Whatever you say, Mills," Georgia said, holding her hands up and surrendering, "but we all know what's going to happen, even if you and Cameron don't."

"Here's my jersey from hockey camp," Millie said as she held it up, attempting to change the conversation from her and Cameron's non-existent relationship.

"And this is the hockey medal from our first championship win!" Georgia shouted, "Oh, there's an actual team photo of us. Look! Look how small we were. Wow, we were all so tiny. It feels like it wasn't so long ago. I didn't realize how much we've grown up."

"I still remember when I met you for the first time at minis, and I used to think you were so mean," Millie said laughing.

"I'm still mean," Georgia said menacingly, "but not to you. So, you are safe. For now, anyway!"

"True, and let's hope it stays that way."

"Preston," Cameron said after he finished slicing a golf ball off into the trees, never to be seen again, "I'm not going to lie. I don't think I'm a natural athlete at all sports, after all. Especially golf. I'm pretty sure that I've also lost us like a dozen golf balls at least."

"At least," Rhys agreed.

"A natural what at what?" Preston replied, confused. "What are you talking about, Cam?"

"Nothing," Cameron laughed, "wrong person. But, I'm rubbish at golf. Thanks for carrying me."

"My shoulders are getting pretty sore now that you mention it," Rhys chimed in.

"Please," Hunter said, "if your shoulders are sore, Preston's must be worn down to the bone because he's been carrying this team all morning!"

The boys were almost to the last hole, and despite a strong start and Preston's best efforts to carry the entire team, with Hunter and Rhys also adding a couple of decent shots, they were still falling short of being able to beat the dads who were currently on the hole ahead of them.

"Come on, gentlemen, last hole. Let's pick up the pace. We've got dinner reservations. Losers pay?" Cameron's dad shouted, getting a few laughs from the other dads.

"We don't have any money," Cameron shouted back, "unless you give it to us!"

"Good point, but hurry up anyway, you bunch of freeloaders. There's another group behind you."

"AREN'T WE ALL a little bit fancy today?" Georgia said, giving her best impression of the Queen by throwing in a royal wave as she looked around the group of girls and their moms at the beauty salon.

"So posh, Georgia dear," Millie replied laughing, "the boys would be completely out of place here."

"Maybe Preston could pull it off," Georgia agreed, "or Hunter, but Cameron and Rhys would have gotten us all thrown out by now with their loud open-mouthed chewing."

"Not to mention the burping," Ashlyn said, chiming in, "those disgusting over-the-top exaggerated burps."

"Rhys doesn't burp!" Daylyn said, defending her absent boyfriend. "Well, not much. Okay, he burps, but I'm sure he wouldn't do it here. He's nicer than that."

"As someone who's spent a lot of time with both Cameron and Rhys, I guarantee they would both be burping and chewing loudly. They're not the morning tea types," Millie said laughing, "unlike us: sassy, stylish, and sophisticated."

The girls and their mothers were enjoying a spa day as their graduation day event, similar to what the boys had done with their dads going to play golf. A little bit of a special reward for them all finishing middle school and doing so well.

Starting with a traditional morning tea at one of the fanciest hotels in town, the girls would move on to the next part of the mother-daughter date day. They would follow it up with a spa treatment at the local beauty and nail salon, where they were all getting facials and the full treatment for their nails.

Luckily for the girls, a parent from one of the grades below, Mrs. Keene, had offered up her beauty salon as part of the graduation celebrations.

"It's funny," Khloe said as she leaned over, "you wouldn't think these adorable little cucumber sandwiches and fancy cakes would be enough to fill you up, but I'm full. And that hot chocolate was so good!"

"The hot chocolate may have been the best cup of hot chocolate I've ever had," Lola agreed, "I think it was those little rainbow marshmallows."

"Or the white chocolate-salted caramel dusting they put on the top of the foam," Daylyn added, "that was pretty good too."

"Okay, girls," Georgia's mom interrupted their conversation as she stood up from the long table and put her napkin down. "The first part of our spa day adventure is complete. I hope you enjoyed your morning tea. Be sure to thank the ladies as you leave. Now, we'll be walking down to the salon for the last part of the day. It's only about ten minutes away, and we're booked for about fifteen minutes from now, so we don't want to be late. So, let's get a hustle on and get moving!"

The girls thanked the staff, exiting through the back door, which led out into a large garden area and over an arched white wooden bridge that spanned the small stream running around the restaurant.

"I think this is what England must look like," Georgia said to Millie as they walked, "with streams and meadows and stone walls everywhere. They have the biggest outdoor area here."

"Yeah," Millie agreed, "it's like the background of every one of those romance book covers that Mom reads. You know, with the lady in the fancy dress and small umbrella thing."

"A parasol," Georgia added, correcting her. "Oh, and don't forget there has to be a shirtless man on horseback or something too." Both girls giggled, linking arms as they walked down the street in the direction of the salon.

When the girls arrived, they found it all set up and the ladies waiting for them.

There was a section for manicures and pedicures, complete with oversized massage chairs, drinks, snacks, and televisions on the wall playing music videos.

"Welcome, girls, and congratulations on your graduation," Mrs. Keene said as they walked around, "the first ten girls, or ladies, can take their place in the massage chairs and get comfortable. The rest of you, head to the next room, and we'll get started on facials."

Georgia and Millie quickly slid into two of the massage chairs, opting for nails first.

"Welcome, girls. My name is Allison, and I'll be your nail technician today. First, do you know what color polish you want?"

"Hi, Allison, my name's Georgia. I brought a swatch from my dress, so if we could do a color that matches that, it would be perfect."

"We certainly can," Allison replied, "and for yourself?" she asked Millie, "do you know what color you want for your polish?"

Millie still couldn't believe that Georgia had been organized enough to bring a swatch of her dress to match her nail color. Why hadn't she thought of that?

"Well, I forgot my dress swatch," Millie lied, "but my dress is that blue color there," she said, pointing at the color chart. "So I was thinking of a pale or light pink."

"I know just the one," Allison said, looking along the wall before picking up a small bottle, "this one?"

"That would be perfect," Millie replied, agreeing, "thank you."

"No worries," Allison replied, "now sit back and relax. I've started the foot massager, so slip your feet into there, and I'll go and grab the nail polish while your feet soak. Here's the remote control for the television. Feel free to pump the music up if it's a song you like."

"This is so cool," Daylyn said, from a couple of chairs down where she sat with her twin, "we should do this more often."

"Think mom would let us come here every week?" Ashlyn asked her sister, "just for a little rest and relaxation, of course."

"Of course," her sister agreed.

"If you two think you need more '*rest and relaxation*' in your life," Janet, their mom, said from the lounge area, "I can think of plenty of things for you to do around the house. I find housework and chores always leave me feeling relaxed afterward."

"What a great idea, Mom," Daylyn said, while looking horrified, "but let's put a pin in that and circle back to it in the future."

"That's what I thought," Janet replied, picking up her magazine and continuing to flick through it, "but the offers are always there y'all."

While Georgia and Millie had their fingernails painted, their feet were soaking in a warm foot wash, and it wasn't long before it was time to get their toenails painted.

With both sets of nails complete, the two girls said goodbye and thank you to Allison and moved over to the other side of the salon where they would get a facial.

It wasn't long before both girls were laid back, their faces covered in some delicious smelling moisturizer mud mix and cucumber slices on their eyes.

"Millie?" Georgia asked.

"Yes?" Millie replied.

"Is this what it feels like to be royalty?" Georgia said, sighing, "it has to."

"Yes. It absolutely does," Millie answered. "This is the life."

For the next couple of hours, the girls and their moms took turns getting their nails done, having face masks and massages, and generally just relaxing and being pampered.

It was the perfect opportunity for the girls to enjoy each other's company as their time together in one school drew close, and they'd all be off to high school.

THE FINAL DAYS of middle school were drawing closer, and all assignments and extra credit activities had been handed in, so the kids were spending their class time watching movies, reading, and, in some cases, playing sports or doing fun outdoor activities.

One of their teachers had even organized a treasure hunt for them, where they had to solve riddles and clues as a team to find the prize at the end. The prize had just been candy and some other miscellaneous stuff, but it was still loads of fun working to gather to solve the puzzles and clues.

Wednesday was their last official day of school, and they had a class party planned, but until then, they still had to show up and be somewhat behaved, although most of the teachers were letting them let off steam and enjoy their final days in a pretty relaxed and chill way.

"Millie," Rhys asked as they left school on Monday afternoon, "you busy this afternoon?"

"No, why?" Millie replied, "what do you wanna do?"

"I'm thinking snacks and video games," Rhys replied, "at my place. Oh, sorry," Rhys said, looking around at his friends, "everyone's invited."

"Sure!" Millie replied. "I'll text Mom and let her know that I'll be home later."

"Bro," Cameron said, "were you even planning on asking me? I'm literally standing right here next to you and spent most of the day with you, and you still didn't mention it."

"No, not really," Rhys said laughing, "because I know you'd say yes anyway. So, I thought I'd just ask everyone else, and you'd show up anyway."

"Fair point," Cameron agreed, "I'll text my mom too."

In the end, Preston and Daylyn ended up joining Rhys, Cameron, and Millie for video games at Rhys's house, and it wasn't long before they got involved in a heated game.

Because of the odd number, they couldn't play two against two, so they were rotating teams.

"Cam, c'mon buddy," Rhys whined, throwing the controller onto the couch, "you are playing like absolute rubbish today. Maybe this is why I didn't

invite you because subconsciously I knew you were going to suck at this game."

"Don't start with me," Cameron fired back, "you left me alone while you ran back to base to grab something. What was I supposed to do?"

"You were supposed to hold it down until I got back," Rhys said, rolling his eyes, "not let Millie and Daylyn take all our stuff!"

"Come on, boys, it's not all bad," Daylyn giggled, "there's always next time."

"She's right," Millie chimed in, "and maybe next time we'll let you have a head start or something. We could give you guys a couple of extra lives or something?"

Millie's phone beeping interrupted her, thankfully for the boys, who had no response to the girls' teasing.

"That's Mom. She's on her way to pick me up, and apparently, she's giving you a ride home too, Cam," Millie said, "so it looks like you are both saved by the bell."

"You have to go too Preston, Daylyn?" Rhys asked, looking around, "or can you stay a little longer? I think Mom's making meatloaf, mashed potato, and gravy for dinner if you both want to hang out and stay for something to eat."

"I'm in no rush. Mom said to call her whenever I'm ready, so I'd love to stay for dinner if that's all right with your mom?" Preston replied.

"Yeah, she already offered," Rhys said, "besides, she makes enough meatloaf to feed the whole neighborhood. Daylyn?"

"I'm good for another hour or so, Mom said, so I'll stay, but you two can play," Daylyn added, "because I think you need more practice than me, Rhys!"

After dropping off Cameron, Millie and her mom were sitting down, eating dinner, and going over her day when her mom dropped a bombshell.

"I have a little bit of a surprise for you."

"What's the surprise?" Millie asked, curious now what her mom had been cooking up behind the scenes.

"Well, I was on the phone this afternoon," her mom began, drawing out this mysterious announcement and milking it for everything it was worth.

"Spit it out already, Mom!" Millie shouted, "You're doing this on purpose now."

"Okay, okay," she said, "your grandparents are coming down for your graduation."

"That's awesome," Millie replied, "are they staying for a while?"

"Yeah, they're going to fly down and spend a couple of days here."

Millie's grandparents lived about eight hours' drive away, so they were choosing to fly down rather than spend the day cramped up in the car. As they'd gotten older, they hadn't been able to visit as much as they had before, so it made every time she got to see them a little more special.

"I knew you'd be happy. Now, help me clean away the dishes and get yourself upstairs to work on your homework."

"Mom, we don't have any more homework," Millie replied, "not for middle school anyway. All my work is handed in and being graded already, but I will go and have a shower. After that, I have to Facetime Mia anyway. It's my turn to call."

"That's so cool your grandparents will get to see you at graduation," Mia said, "I wish I could be there with you guys."

Millie hadn't failed to notice that during the call, whenever they'd talked about the upcoming graduation, Mia had seemed a little bit down. It must have been hard having to graduate at a new school with kids that she hadn't spent most of her school years with. However, with how often Mia and her parents moved, she hadn't really spent more than a couple of years at any one school or city.

"I wish you'd be at graduation with us, Mia," Millie said, "it won't be the same without you."

"I know," Mia replied, "sorry, I've been a bit down about the whole graduation thing. I'm really happy for you all, and it's not like I don't have friends here for my own graduation, but it's, I don't know, I'm just a bit sad about it is all."

"I get that, and I understand. I wouldn't want to graduate somewhere new, either. I just want to fly down there and steal you away!"

"That would be hilarious," Mia replied, "but I'm sure my parents would come and hunt me down after how much I spent on my graduation dress!"

"Oh, was it expensive, and do you have it yet?" Millie said, clapping, "Show me!"

"It was," Mia said, smiling, "and I do. I think Mom was feeling a little bit guilty about the whole thing, so she went all out on my dress. Do you have yours?"

"Of course, Mom picked it up this morning. Let's do a dress show!" Millie said, clapping before she laughed. *Who'd have thought that I would get excited about trying on dresses,* Millie thought. *Maybe I am growing up?*

IT WAS THE last official day of school for eighth grade, and there were a lot of mixed emotions. While many of the kids were happy that school was over for another year, they also knew that things were about to change.

For many of the Dakota kids, this would be their last year of school together. For others, they would get to continue on to high school together, and there was always hockey, lacrosse, and other sports, but many relationships would undeniably be changed forever.

Instead of morning classes, the teachers and families had organized a party with board games, movies, food, and music. They'd opened up the partition divide between two classes, with music in one room and movies and board games in the other.

SAM LAWRENCE & BEN JACKSON

DJ Rhys, as he had been referring to himself all morning, was in charge of playing music, and he'd been taking his role very seriously.

"Who has a song request?" Rhys shouted over the top of the music blasting out of the speakers in front of him, his large headphones half on and half off his head. "If you know the name, write it down on the sheet. If you don't know the name, I'll try my best to figure it out."

From the other classroom, Cameron and Hunter were talking.

As the only two remaining players of a heated game of Monopoly, they were battling each other to see who would emerge victorious. Like most games of Monopoly, it had turned into an epic battle between wealthy tycoons, with neither hurting the other enough to land a victory blow.

"He's right into that DJ role," Hunter said, shaking his head as another dance remix started to blast out of the speakers.

"Right? But are you surprised?" Cameron agreed. "Every time we have a party or gathering, and there's music there, Rhys finds a way to take over as the DJ."

"True," Hunter said, "we should have expected it. Remember at my party when my mom hired that

DJ, and somehow, Rhys was still up there playing music within the first hour?"

"That was hilarious," Cameron laughed, "that DJ had no idea what was happening. Some random kid from the party starts advising them on what songs to play and how to mix."

"Isn't this game over with yet?" Khloe asked, looking over their shoulders at the vast array of hotels and houses spread out all over the board.

"Almost," Hunter said, "your boy just lost his train stations, and I've got my eye on that street full of juicy little houses next. I'm going to bulldoze them and put down some hotels once I get my hands on those little beauties. Time to take that residential street to the next level with the right type of management."

"It was an unlucky roll," Cameron said, rolling his eyes, "he got lucky, but he is kind of in a good position right now. I'm running out of safe places to land."

"Well, once you're done," Khloe asked, "let me know. I want to play next. I haven't played Monopoly for years. Almost forgot how fun it was."

"Oh, when this game is done, and Cameron's broke," Hunter said, "we'll go again. I'm feeling lucky!"

"The game would go a lot faster without all the chirping," Cameron grumbled.

"Oh, less chirping," Hunter said, laughing and slapping his thigh, "I remember a certain someone was very '*chirpy*' themselves not so long ago. What was his name? Hmm. I forget, but it doesn't matter. That person won't be around for much longer, and he's been a lot quieter for the last ten minutes."

"Roll the dice, bro," Cameron said, shaking his head, "just roll the dice already."

"Okay," Georgia said, "I think that's everyone I wanted to say goodbye to."

Georgia, Millie, Daylyn, and Ashlyn had been touring around the school, dropping in on some of the younger kids' classes to say goodbye to the girls and boys they were friends with that were in the grades below them.

"It's almost lunchtime," Ashlyn said, looking at her phone, "we should get back to class for the party."

"Good idea," Millie agreed, "I didn't realize how hungry I was getting. I probably should have eaten breakfast this morning instead of just grabbing a granola bar to eat on the way to school."

"Maybe," Georgia began, as the friends started walking, "just maybe, if you set your alarm for ten minutes earlier, you would have time to sit and eat breakfast like all the rest of us instead of being late every morning. No offense, but—"

"This is 100% going to be offensive," Millie interrupted, "whenever someone says no offense, but it's always offensive."

"I don't know how Cameron put up with you being late every morning for all these years," Georgia finished, "I would have whipped you into shape in no time at all. Have you up bright and early with the birds."

"I'll have you know, Georgia," Millie replied, putting a long and drawn-out emphasis on her best friend's name, "that I'm not late every day. I just enjoy my beauty sleep."

"You are kind of the last one ready all the time, Mills," Ashlyn added, "sorry."

"Oh, I see how it is," Millie said, rolling her eyes dramatically, "the last day and my friends are all turning against me. All alone, I wander the halls. Not a friend in sight, destined to be the last one to arrive anywhere. Forever known as that '*late girl*' who doesn't know how to set an alarm clock."

"Yeah, yeah. Let's try and take the drama down just a notch," Georgia said, "your majesty. If that's at all possible. Now, let's go eat before all the good party foods are taken. Besides, maybe they saved something for us because of, you know."

"Because of what?" Millie asked.

"Because we're with the '*late girl*,' that's why," Georgia said, laughing before running away up the hall.

Despite the party atmosphere, it was a subdued group of friends that sat down together to eat lunch.

"I just realized that this is the last day that we'll all sit down together and eat lunch at this school," Georgia said quietly, "and I might actually miss this school and the teachers."

"Same," Millie agreed, "who knows what our new teachers and school are going to be like?"

"Most of us still play hockey together," Cameron added, trying to lift the mood a little, "and do other stuff. Not to mention, a lot of us will be in the same high school. So, it's not like we're not going to see each other."

"True," Daylyn agreed, "but still, it won't be the same."

It was a day of mixed emotions. Happiness about finishing middle school and moving on to high school, but also sadness and nervousness about change, and this emotional roller coaster wasn't quite over yet.

"Get in my photo!" Millie shouted to someone across the quad area before disappearing into the crowd of kids, all trying to get photos with one another for the last time out in front of the school.

Once the final bell rang, the graduating class streamed out of their classroom, cheering and shouting as they made their way for the final time out of their classroom. However, all good things had to come to an end, and slowly, parents showed up to collect their kids, and others made their way home on foot.

Their last day of middle school was officially over.

"I keep getting all emotional," Georgia said, "school is over."

"Until we start high school," Millie added, "then it's a new school and maybe even new friends."

"I don't want to make new friends," Georgia whined, "the ones I have are already so much hard work. I just don't know if I have the time or energy to make new friends. Who has the time for all that drama?"

"Please," Millie said, throwing a cushion at her friend sitting across the room, "being best friends with you is no picnic either."

Millie and Georgia were having a sleepover before going to get their hair done in the morning. However, between the two of them, the mood was pretty subdued.

"Think about it this way, there's probably a bunch of new people to meet. New friends and cute boys. We also have a new hockey team to try out for, which will be fun," Millie said, trying to cheer Georgia up.

"True," Georgia agreed, "plus new outfits. Mom said she'd take me shopping for some new clothes before school starts, so that's a bonus."

"See," Millie said, "you have to look on the bright side."

"But speaking of cute boys," Georgia grinned, "how are you and Cam?"

Despite her best efforts, Millie blushed. She just couldn't help herself. "We're fine. Just taking things slowly, and honestly, nothing much has changed between us. We're still best friends, but there is this kind of other element there now, too."

"I have to admit that seeing y'all as anything other than best friends would take a little getting used to. Regardless of how cute and adorable you two are."

"Yeah, but I think that's why whatever happens if anything happens, it needs to happen slowly. There's too much at stake to rush into it," Millie replied, "the last thing either of us wants to do is ruin our friendship again. Even though we were only little at the time, it wasn't a whole lot of fun for anyone."

Both girls spent the rest of the evening talking, watching movies, and doing TikTok dances together in their pajamas late into the night before eventually falling asleep.

GRADUATION DAY WAS finally here! Thanks to how excited she was, Millie had wakened up bright and early without the need to set an alarm.

"Let's go, Georgia," Millie said, waking her bestie up, "it's graduation day!"

"Remind me again why we're friends," Georgia whined, rolling over and putting her pillow over her face. "It's so early, Mills!"

"The early bird gets the worm, Georgia," Millie said laughing, "and we've got a lot of stuff we need to get done – hair, makeup, photos, and so on."

"Just five more minutes," Georgia replied. "I'm begging you."

"Oh, good. You're both awake," Millie's mom said, poking her head in through the doorway, "breakfast is almost ready, so come down when-ever you want to eat."

"Thanks, Mom," Millie replied, "once I get Grumpy up, we'll both be down."

The girls both went to the bathroom, brushed their teeth, and headed downstairs for breakfast. Before Millie even made it, she could tell by the smell of freshly cooked pancakes what they were having, and so could Georgia, whose nose was leading the way.

"Mrs. Duncan, I mean Patty," Georgia said, correcting herself before Millie's mom did, "this all smells delicious and more than makes up for the early wake-up call."

"You're welcome, Georgia," Patty said, smiling, "a nice plate of bacon and pancakes is enough to get anyone out of bed bright and early. You girls have your hair appointment at one o'clock, then you're coming back here to start getting ready. Georgia, your mom is either going to meet us at the hairdresser or back here, she's not sure yet. After that, we have photos, and then it'll be time to head over to your grad ceremony. So, you have a few hours to relax, but first get your dresses out and have them hanging somewhere, just to make sure there's no wrinkles or anything we need to adjust."

"Okay, Mom," Millie replied, stuffing a mouthful of maple syrup-covered hot pancake and bacon into her mouth, "thanks."

It was a few hours later in the park down the road where Cameron, Preston, Rhys, and Hunter were lazily throwing a lacrosse ball back and forth, seeing who could do the best trick passes and shots.

"What do you think the girls are doing?" Hunter asked, passing Cameron the ball behind his back.

"Millie said they're going to get their hair done soon, then after that, they have to do their makeup and then get dressed ready for photos," Cameron replied, "not having fun like us."

"That's for sure," Rhys said, tossing the ball up high in the air before losing it in the sun and diving out of the way, "look out!"

The four boys scattered, running and laughing, with the lacrosse ball thudding down between them and missing Cameron by less than a foot before rolling away.

"Bro!" Cameron shouted, "you could have concussed me!"

"I think you're more worried about your hair than a concussion," Rhys replied smirking. "Imagine what Millie would think if you showed up with a big gash on your face or something."

"Shut it, buddy," Cameron shot back, "before you end up being the one with a gash on your face, and then you'll have to explain that to *your* girlfriend."

"As fun as this is," Hunter replied, "I think the pizza we ordered for lunch will be at your place by now, Cam. We should probably start heading back. Otherwise, it's going to be cold."

"Good point," Preston agreed, "plus I'm starving anyway."

As the boys started walking home, they discussed what they needed to do to get ready, and it was a lot less than the girls. Teeth brushing, a shower, and a quick change, and they'd be ready to rock and roll, according to Rhys.

All the kids would be getting into their suits and dresses at home, but they'd been allowed to bring their gowns home with them on the last day of school so they could throw them on just before the ceremony.

Five minutes later, the four boys were walking up Cameron's drive when the pizza guy jumped in his car and left.

"Perfect timing," Cameron's dad said, taking a bite of a slice of pizza, "Pizza's here. What, could you smell it from the park or something?"

"Something like that," Cameron said laughing, "plus Hunter's stomach was growling so loud the ladies walking their dogs around thought there was a wolf loose in the park. So, we had to leave."

"Funny guy," Hunter said, "but it's not like you're not all hungry too. I'm just the only one with half a brain that remembered that we ordered pizza."

"Don't you girls just look fantastic!" Georgia's mom said, as the two girls walked up the driveway, "They did an awesome job with your hair."

"So, they should have," Millie's mom replied, "for how long we just spent there. Almost two hours for hair. It's crazy how long it takes. I forgot how long hair takes. I need to get my hair done and go out more often."

"Don't we all," Georgia's mom said laughing, "we spend all of our money on these kids and all our free time at hockey tournaments or in stinky arenas."

"Okay, girls," Millie's mom said, looking at her watch, "we have an hour or so for makeup and to get dressed before Cameron and his family arrive, so let's get a hustle on."

Cameron was as nervous as he could ever remember being as he walked up the front path to Millie's house. With every step, he felt more and more nervous, and he couldn't help but tug on his tie, which currently felt as if it were strangling him.

"Stop messing with it, mate," Cameron's dad said, "otherwise we'll just need to redo it."

"It feels too tight," Cameron replied.

"It's a tie," his dad replied, "it's supposed to feel tight. You're not wearing a necklace."

Just as he was about to knock on the door, it swung open, and Millie was standing there smiling at him.

"Wow," Cameron said, looking at Millie in her dress with her makeup and hair done, "Umm, you, look—"

"Amazing? Beautiful? Stunning?" Millie offered. "Is that what you were going to say?"

"All three," Cameron said, agreeing. "You look great, Mills."

"Thank you," Millie replied, blushing, "you scrub up pretty good yourself, Cam."

"Don't you look just smashing, Cameron," Millie's mom said, standing behind Millie in the doorway. "Well, don't just leave everyone stand-ing outside, Millie. Invite them in. Let's get this party started."

The next hour was spent with family photos, group photos, Millie and Cameron photos, and just about every type of photo you could imagine in every possible pose and location before they finally loaded themselves into cars and headed off to their graduation ceremony.

10

THE OFFICIAL GRADUATION ceremony was being held in the large auditorium at the community center right next to the school. Because the gym in the school was relatively small, anytime they had anything significant with a lot of visitors, it was easier just to hold it at the community center.

After the ceremony, the kids would all head down to the large hall, which had been decorated by the seventh grade kids and their parents for their graduation party.

As the kids arrived, dressed in their caps and gowns, they milled around outside while the parents, other family members, and guests went inside to be seated.

"Okay, kids," Mr. Smith said, hushing them all, "let's try to keep the noise down to a dull roar. I know you all know your alphabet by now. If you don't, I've done a terrible job teaching you. But in case anyone forgets, there's a list in alphabetical order stuck right here next to me on the door."

The kids walked into the small waiting room and lined themselves up alphabetically. Once everyone else was seated, they would walk into the auditorium and sit in order, to make it easier when their names were called.

"I'm so nervous," Millie whispered to Daylyn, "but I don't know why."

"Same," Daylyn replied, "but it'll be fine once we get up there. At least you don't have to give a speech."

"Shush," Ashlyn hissed, "I'm trying not to think about the speech."

"Okay, everyone," Mr. Smith announced, "it's time to go."

As the kids walked from the small room and into the auditorium, all the guests stood and applauded, with cameras flashing all over the place.

"Now I know what it's like to be a celebrity with the paparazzi snapping photos of you," Georgia whispered.

Once the kids were seated, Mrs. Keenan, their principal, stood at the podium and waited for the noise to gradually stop.

"Welcome, everyone! It's a pleasure to see all of you here today to celebrate with our graduating class. I'll keep my speech short. I know that you're not here to listen to me chatter away, and we'll get straight into the awards, which will be handed out by the teachers. Over the last few years, it's been my pleasure to teach, observe, and mentor this fantastic group of kids. Seeing their growth and maturity blossom over the years has really been special. I know when I say this, I say it on behalf of all their teachers and the rest of the staff. Thank you for the hard work that you've all put in, and I wish you all the best in the future. Now, before the awards presentation starts, let's give them a big round of applause."

The parents and families all stood up and gave the graduating class a rousing round of applause before retaking their seats.

"Thank you," Mrs. Keenan said, waiting for the noise to quiet down again before continuing. "We have four awards to give out today. The first is the community award, followed by the STEM and athletics awards. The final award will be our Valedictorian award. Mr. Smith will be coming up next to announce the winner of the community award."

"Thank you, Mrs. Keenan. Our community award for this year is awarded to a student who has shown exemplary dedication to her local

SAM LAWRENCE & BEN JACKSON

community, including our school community. This year's winner of the community award is Lisa Taylor!" Mr. Smith said, standing back from the podium to clap as Lisa made her way up to the stage to accept her award and give a small speech.

"Thank you, Mr. Smith. Next up, we have our STEM award, which will be handed out by Miss Franks," Mrs. Keenan said, handing the microphone over to Miss Franks.

"Thanks, Principal Keenan. Our Science, Technology, Engineering, and Mathematics award for this year goes to a student who has excelled in STEM, Lin Lee!"

After another short speech, it was time for the announcement of the athletics award, which was typically awarded to a boy and girl who had both excelled in physical activity and sports. The physical education teacher, Mrs. Grant, took the stage to announce this year's winners.

"I'm proud to announce that this year's winners for the sports and athletics award are Millie Duncan and Cameron Simonds for their good sportsmanship, commitment to physical activity, and positive attitude!"

Millie and Cameron looked at one another, and their jaws dropped. Neither had expected to win an award tonight, let alone one together, so it was two very shocked kids who walked up to the stage to accept their awards, accompanied by clapping and cheering from the kids and families gathered in the audience.

After shaking Mrs. Grant's hand and accepting their framed certificates, Millie nudged a reluctant Cameron toward the microphone.

"Thank you, Mrs. Grant and the rest of the staff. I guess I'm giving the speech on behalf of both of us. Umm, I really wasn't expecting an award, so I didn't have anything prepared, but here we go. We both love playing sports – lacrosse, hockey, and just about anything else – so to receive an award because of that is really cool. So, thank you, I guess, and well done to us!"

After Millie and Cameron had their photos taken, they left the stage, and Mrs. Keenan returned to announce the final award, Valedictorian. Because of the announcement at school, most of the kids already knew who it was going to be.

"While this one isn't a surprise, it's undeniably one of my favorite awards to give out each year. Thanks to her hard work, attention to detail, and dedication to her academic pursuits, Ashlyn Johnson, you're this year's Valedictorian! Well done!"

Ashlyn left her seat and made her way up to the stage where she received her award, shook Mrs. Keenan's hand, and had her photo taken before she was passed the microphone.

"First, thank you to all the teachers and faculty members who nominated me for Valedictorian. Just like myself, I'll keep this speech short," Ashlyn said, her joke getting a laugh from the assembled crowd and allowing her to relax before she continued. "I wasn't always a perfect student and I'm not perfect all the time, but what I lack in perfection I make up for in ambition. I always strive to not only be the best but be the best version of myself and put 110% effort into everything I do. So, you may not be the best right now, but if you work hard and stay true to yourself, you'll always do well. Thank you again to the staff, my friends, and most importantly, my mom and stepdad. I love you both, and thanks for always supporting me and encouraging me to be the best version of myself."

Ashlyn left the stage to a standing ovation, with her mom Janet and Coach Phil, her stepdad both in tears.

Mrs. Keenan announced that they would be handing out diplomas next. She would be calling the kids one at a time to receive their diploma, there would be a short pause for photos, and then the next student would be called.

As the kids took turns receiving their diplomas, they shook Mrs. Keenan's hand, switched their tassels from the right side of their cap to the left, had their photos taken, and then headed back to their seats.

Once the last student had received his diploma, Mrs. Keenan took to the stage for the final farewell speech, wishing each of the kids the best in life and thanking them for their hard work and school spirit.

"And again, thank you all. It's been a pleasure teaching you all, and on behalf of the rest of the staff at Dakota Middle School, we wish the graduating class all the best."

After the noise of the rousing standing ovation had dwindled, Mrs. Keenan explained that the kids would be outside the auditorium for a class photo together. They were free to do any family photos before returning their gowns and heading to the hall for their graduation party.

THE PARENTS FOLLOWED the kids to the party next door but didn't stay long, except for a few chaperones, leaving them to enjoy their graduation party. No sooner had the parents left than the lights dimmed, and the DJ fired off the first song of the evening, calling all the kids to the dance floor.

For the most part, the kids clustered in groups around the edge of the large hall, nervously looking at the empty dance floor and listening to the DJ trying to coax them out onto it.

It took a few minutes for the kids to make their way onto the dance floor as no one wanted to be the first one to make a move, but eventually, a couple of kids decided to start dancing. Soon, a trickle of kids became a flood as they all rushed onto the dance floor.

Dakota Middle School Graduation

One song ended, and the DJ switched to the most popular song of the year, and now even the final holdouts, who hadn't decided to dance yet, stood up.

"Let's go, Millie," Cameron said, standing up from their table and holding his hand out to her, "time to dance. I know you love this song."

Almost fifteen minutes later, most of their table had been out and danced before returning to their table to have a drink and rest for a minute.

While they were resting, the DJ announced to the crowd of kids that it was time to slow things down and switched to some slower songs.

Rhys, who'd been having a break from dancing, grabbed Daylyn's hand and dragged her, laughing and giggling, back out on the dance floor for round two. Hunter, seeing this, asked Georgia if she'd like to dance, Preston asked Ashlyn, and Khloe and Logan looked at each other before bursting out laughing.

"Come on, Khloe," Logan said, standing up, "us goalies stick together. Let's show them how real dancers dance!"

Finally, it was just Cameron and Millie left sitting at the table. Everyone else had already headed back out onto the dance floor for round two.

Raising his voice to be heard over the music, Cameron cleared his throat before beginning, "I know we were out there before," he said, motioning to the dance floor, "but would you like to dance with me, Millie Duncan?"

Millie was nervous. This wasn't just dancing on the dance floor with a bunch of her friends. This was dancing slow and close, just her and Cameron. "Um, sure. I'd love to," she replied, standing and arranging her dress.

As the pair slowly started to dance, Millie looked around and noticed that a lot of the kids dancing next to them were watching her and Cameron.

"Everyone's looking at us," Millie tried to tell Cameron over the sound of the music.

"What did you say?" Cameron asked, confused, not hearing her because of the loud music. He leaned in closer to better hear what she was saying as Millie leaned in to repeat what she'd said.

In that moment, the two were possibly as close to one another as they'd ever been.

Millie smiled at Cameron, forgetting all about what she'd been trying to say, and kissed him before giggling and pulling back. For his part, Cameron was shocked. Standing there with his mouth hanging open like a fish.

What the pair hadn't realized was that if all the kids on the dance floor hadn't been looking at them before, they certainly were now. The slow song ended, and the DJ switched it up again as the kids filtered off the dance floor and back to their tables.

"Umm, Mills," Georgia asked, grabbing her friend by the elbow, "come to the bathroom with me."

No sooner had the pair left the main hall than Georgia spun around and confronted her best friend, "Did you just kiss Cam in the middle of the dance floor, or am I hallucinating?"

"I think I did," Millie said, laughing and blushing again, "I don't know what I was thinking. One minute, we were trying to talk to each other over the top of the music. The next thing I knew, I just went for it. I don't know what came over me. Hopefully, he doesn't get all weirded out by the kiss."

"I don't think he's going to be weirded out," Georgia said, looking through the small glass panel on the door into the hall, "in fact, he looks pretty happy about the current situation."

Back at the table, Cameron was surrounded by the rest of the group, all looking at him and waiting for him to say something. He hadn't said a single thing since he'd sat down after returning from the dance floor.

"What?" he asked, looking at everyone just staring at him, "what is everyone looking at?"

"Dude," Rhys finally said, "are you really sitting there saying nothing after what we all just witnessed?"

"What do you mean?" Cameron replied, "the kiss?"

"This guy. I swear," Rhys shot straight back, rolling his eyes, "of course, the kiss. What else happened on the dance floor that any of us would possibly care about or want to talk about. How do you feel about it, seeing as you guys were supposed to be just friends?"

"I'm not sure," Cameron replied, "it hasn't really sunk in yet."

As they were talking, Millie and Georgia returned to the table, sliding into their seats and interrupting the conversation. All eyes were on their table, and several of the surrounding tables were looking at the pair.

Millie and Cameron were definitely the big topic of conversation at the dance that evening.

Millie looked at Cameron and smiled, and Cameron smiled back.

"Who said goalies were uncoordinated," Khloe said, sliding down into her seat after reenacting some of the strangest dance moves the group of kids had ever seen, "did you see those dance moves out there on the dance floor? Logan and I were smashing it."

Millie leaned over close to Cameron and whispered in his ear, "We'll talk later." Cameron nodded.

For the next couple of hours, the kids all danced, laughed, and took selfies together. It wasn't long before it was time to wrap things up, and the parents began arriving at the hall to pick up their kids.

Millie, Cameron, Rhys, Hunter, and Georgia were all being picked up and driven home by Georgia's mom.

As the kids all piled into the large SUV, talking and chatting about the dance, Millie and Cameron found themselves sitting next to one another in the back row of the vehicle.

In the darkness of the car, Cameron tried to reach for his phone in his pocket and instead brushed his hand against Millie's hand on the seat next to him. He jerked his hand away, then thought *who cares*, and slowly took Millie's hand, squeezing it.

Millie smiled in the darkness, squeezing his hand in return.

Eventually, it was Cameron's turn to be dropped off, leaving just Millie and Georgia in the car.

"Thank you for the ride home, Mrs. Stanford," Cameron said, climbing over the seat, "goodnight, Georgia and Millie, I'll text you when I get home."

"You're welcome, Cameron," Georgia's mom replied, "anytime."

Millie jumped over the seat in front of her so she could sit closer to Georgia. Now, it was just her and Georgia left. They chatted back and forth about the dance and graduation but didn't talk about anything important. Millie was spending the night at Georgia's house, so they could wait until they were home and settled to talk more about the night's events.

Once the two girls had showered and changed into their pajamas, they finally found a moment to sit down and talk to one another.

"So, Miss Kiss," Georgia began, "did you get a chance to talk to Cameron about the kiss?"

"No. Not really," Millie replied, "but we held hands too in the car on the way home."

"Wow, anything else you're not telling me? Any other moves planned that I should know about?" Georgia said, rolling her eyes.

"This is the first chance I've had to talk to you," Millie said, "so you can stop with the eye rolling already. The kiss wasn't planned. It just sort of happened. You know?"

"Yeah, I get it," Georgia said, stretching out on her bed. "So, are you two officially boyfriend and girlfriend now?"

"We haven't talked about it," Millie replied, as a ding on her phone signaled that she'd received a text, "speak of the devil."

"Ooh," Georgia said, trying to look at the screen over her best friend's shoulder, "what does it say?"

"He just said that he had a nice night and was glad that everything happened, and we'd talk more about it tomorrow," Millie replied, "and goodnight."

"What a romantic," Georgia said, laughing, receiving a pillow in the face from Millie in return for her efforts.

"Stop it," Millie said, "it was nice of him to text. Look, I don't know what's going to happen between Cameron and me, but he's my best friend, and he always will be. If that's just the first kiss we ever share or the last, I'll be happy with whatever we decide."

12

"MY LEGS ARE so sore," Georgia whined over the top of her bowl of fruit salad and yogurt the following day as Millie and she sat together eating, "I need a massage."

"You need to stretch," Millie replied laughing, "we both do. Not like we go dancing like that every day."

"True," Georgia replied, "I can't believe school is finally finished. Kind of sad."

"Excited and nervous too," Millie agreed, "but yeah, still sad."

"What are you doing the rest of the day, Mills? Do you have any plans?"

"My grandparents stayed over last night," Millie replied, "so I'm going to spend some time with them this morning before they head home, but I think the rest of my day is wide open if you come up with anything."

As Millie and Georgia talked, making plans to catch up later at the park, she checked her phone and saw a message from Cameron. She told him she'd be home in an hour or so if he wanted to come over, or they could meet up at the park.

"See you later!" Georgia shouted out the window of her mom's car as they drove away from Millie's house. "Text me!"

"I will!" Millie shouted back laughing, before turning around, confused, to find Cameron waiting for her on her front porch.

"Hey, Mills. Sorry, I know that we were going to meet at the park later. Your grandparents are here, but I just wanted to chat first," Cameron said as Millie sat down next to him on the porch.

"That's okay, no worries. Come in. I'll say hi to Mom and Dad and my grandparents, then we can go and hang out."

"Cool," Cameron replied, "as long as your parents will be okay with that?"

"They'll be fine. Let's go in already."

After Millie had reintroduced Cameron to her grandparents and spent some time talking and hanging out, talking about the dance and the graduation ceremony, Cameron and Millie made their way downstairs to the basement.

"Oh, before you go out this afternoon, remember that we still have to do your grad gift tonight at some point," Millie's mom said.

"I forgot," Millie replied, "what is it that I'm getting again?"

"Nice try, buster," her mom answered laughing, "you'll need to wait and find out."

Making their way downstairs, both kids sat on the couch, not talking.

The silence was deafening until Millie started to giggle, and once she started, she couldn't stop, her giggles turning into uncontrollable laughter until tears began rolling down her cheeks.

"What has got into you?" Cameron asked, confused about what was happening. "Did I miss the joke? What's so funny?"

"I was just laughing at us," Millie replied, drying her eyes, "when have either of us just sat not talking to one another in our entire lives?"

"You're right," Cameron said laughing, "but this is unknown territory for us. I'm not sure where we go from here or what we're doing."

"How about this," Millie began, "Cameron Simonds, would you like to be my boyfriend?"

Cameron didn't know how to respond; his mouth was just falling open, his lips were moving, and no words were coming out. *This isn't how things are meant to go,* he thought. He'd made his way over to Millie's house this morning with the intention of trying to convince her that they should date, and now she'd completely surprised him by suggesting exactly what he wanted.

"Millie Duncan, we've always been best friends, and regardless of what happens between us, we always will be. I would love to be your boyfriend."

"We're really doing this?" Millie asked, holding out her hand.

"I guess we're really doing it," Cameron replied, taking Millie's hand. "Do you think the rest of the gang is ready for this?"

"One hundred percent not," Millie said giggling, "and that reminds me," she said, taking out her phone, "if I don't update Georgia first, and someone else tells her, or we arrive at the park after holding hands, she will disown me."

The two spent the next hour playing video games together while the rest of their friends got organized and managed to finally arrange a time to meet at the park.

While they were waiting, Millie snuck a photo of her holding Cameron's hand and sent it to Georgia along with a message saying she'd fill her in at the park. Georgia replied with multiple exclamations and a love heart emoji.

When they both walked upstairs and said good-bye to Millie's parents on the way out the door, Millie's mom thought Millie looked exceptionally happy. She was expecting her to be a little down about school being finished but was pleasantly surprised to see her smiling as if she'd just won a prize.

After they shut the door, Millie's mom, Patty, looked out the front window and watched the two kids take each other's hand before heading to the park.

"Brian!" she shouted to her husband, "You're not going to believe this, but I think Cameron and Millie are dating. They just walked down the road holding hands."

"Surprised it took so long," her husband, replied, not looking up from the newspaper he was reading.

"True," Patty replied, "things will be different around here now, that's for sure."

Millie and Cameron walked hand in hand through the gate and down the path toward the basketball courts, where the rest of the kids were waiting for them. Of all the kids, it was Georgia who noticed them first, quickly telling everyone to check out who'd finally decided to join them.

There are a lot of shocked expressions, and not a lot of talking as Millie and Cameron made their way up to the group.

"What's up, guys?" Cameron said, looking around, "What's going on?" he looked over his shoulder assuming everyone was looking at him.

"Umm, what's up with you guys?" Rhys said, looking down at Cameron and Millie holding hands, then back up at Cameron with a confused look on his face.

"Oh," Cameron said, looking down at Millie's hand in his, "I forgot about this."

"We're officially dating," Millie said, "so get used to it. But surely you can't all be surprised."

"Surprised, yes," Ashlyn replied, "shocked a little, yes. It's like we've all been waiting for this to happen for so long and expecting it, but it never did. So, we all sort of gave up on it. You guys do look pretty cute together, though. Congratulations!"

After Ashlyn said congratulations, the rest of the kids finally found their voices, and there was a round of clapping and congratulations and good luck from all the friends.

"Okay, okay," Cameron said, "enough about us. Are we going to play some basketball or what?"

Preston's house was once again the venue of choice for the kids and their parents, with a big BBQ and pool session, which was the perfect way for all the kids to hang out and relive their graduation and the party afterward.

For Millie and Cameron, it was their first party as boyfriend and girlfriend, and even Georgia commented on how cute they were and how they hadn't left each other's side the whole night.

Finally, it was time to go, and Millie's mom arrived to pick her up at the party. She'd been spending the day with her parents, so she had decided not to attend.

"Hi, Mom," Millie said, climbing into the car, "thanks for picking me up."

"You're welcome," her mom replied, "but first, do you have something to tell me, Millie Duncan?"

"Umm, no?" Millie replied, confused.

"Don't play shy with me, miss. I saw Cameron, and you walk out of the house and down the street holding hands today and looking at each other with those big puppy dog eyes."

"Oh, that," Millie said laughing. "Let me tell you the whole story..."

13

"MILLIE?" HER MOM shouted from downstairs. "Have you got a minute?"

"Coming, Mom," Millie shouted back, putting her phone down and heading downstairs to the kitchen, where she assumed her mom was waiting for her.

"Oh hey," her mom said when she walked in, "last night with the news of you and Cameron, I completely forgot your graduation gift, but rest assured, I haven't forgotten."

"That's okay, Mom. I knew you wouldn't have forgotten completely. Honestly, all this mystery and suspense makes the whole thing pretty exciting."

"Well, that's good news then," her mom said laughing, "perhaps we should make you wait longer for all your presents from now on?"

"I think that could be a little excessive," Millie replied smiling, "let's not get carried away."

"Fair enough. Oh, don't forget you have a surprise with the other kids today at the arena."

"Now you have to tell me what this is about," Millie began, "none of us have been able to figure it out. Even Georgia doesn't know what's going on, and she's the biggest snoop of all."

"Like the other surprise," her mom said, smirking, "you'll have to wait and see!"

"Congratulations on your graduation, Cam," his parents said, as he sat eating breakfast that morning, "we're both very proud of you."

"Thanks, Mom. Thanks, Dad."

"Before your surprise at the arena, we wanted to give you a little gift. Just our way of saying we're proud of what a good job you did this year," his dad said, handing him a small envelope.

"Thanks, but you didn't have to," Cameron said, opening the envelope. "Oh, awesome. A season pass to the amusement park. We were all talking about getting one of these for the summer. And a receipt?"

"Yeah, we know you're trying to save some of your money, so we deposited some money into your savings account also," his mom said, "you don't have to save it all, but we thought we'd kick-start the account a little."

Cameron wanted to start a part-time job, and over the summer, he was planning on mowing lawns and doing odd jobs around the neighborhood, so eventually, he could buy a car once he got his license.

"Thanks again, guys," Cameron said, giving both his parents a hug, "you guys are awesome."

As Millie got out of the car at the arena later that day, she had a confused look on her face, which matched her general confusion about this entire surprise. *What on earth are we doing here?*

"Don't forget your hockey bag, Millie," her mom said, opening the trunk and revealing Millie's hockey equipment and stick.

"What? Why do you have my hockey bag? Is the surprise we're playing hockey?" she asked, even more confused.

"You'll have to wait and see. Now grab your bag and head inside to changing room one."

Millie, more confused than ever, grabbed her bag and headed inside the arena to changing room one, where she discovered the rest of her teammates, all equally confused. Apparently, the boys were also here in changing room three.

"Anyone know what's going on?" she asked, sitting down on the bench to start getting ready.

"Nope," Khloe replied, "no idea. I just got told to get changed and be out on the ice in ten minutes."

The rest of the girls had a similar story, so Millie stopped worrying and instead focussed on getting changed so she wouldn't be late.

"Welcome, kids," boomed a voice over the loudspeaker, "if we could have the boys on one bench and girls on the other, we'll let you know what's going on."

As the kids lined up, whispering to one another, they slowly started to piece it together.

"As a final hoorah, we're going to be recreating the classic boys versus girls, Lightning versus Hurricanes, grudge match," the parent on the announcer said, "and after, free skating followed by the famous Dakota pizza party we've enjoyed for all these seasons. So, players and coaches, get ready, and let's get this game started!"

The game started, reminiscent of their fourth grade grudge match, with all the kids putting in maximum effort, but it wasn't long before it began to get a little silly.

As usual, it was Rhys who started it. Rather than taking a regular shot on the net, he tried a trick shot off Hunter's helmet, bouncing the puck into the net. Well, no sooner had he finished celebrating than the girls recreated the classic Flying V from the movies to attempt their own shot on Logan.

With the score at 5–5, and the kids caring more about trick shots than playing hockey, Coach Phil and Coach John called the game, much to the disappointment of the kids on the ice, eliciting a lot of boos from the benches.

"Stop," Coach John said, "we're going to do a shootout with a twist to determine the winner. We've got some prizes for the best trick shot that goes into the net and also a prize for the goalie that stops the most pucks."

"What are the prizes?" Rhys shouted.

"You'll find out when we give them out, Rhys," Coach Phil said laughing, "but don't worry, we're pretty sure you'll love them."

The kids all lined up at one end of the ice, and the two goalies took their positions at the other end. Each player would get two shots.

The first couple of shots were wild, with nothing finding the back of the net, but it wasn't long before the kids started to get into their groove.

Preston was the first one to nail his trick shot. As he got close to the crease, he flicked the puck up onto the side of the blade, twirled it around in one smooth motion, and then flicked it towards the top left corner of the net for a goal.

The parents spectating, and the kids, went crazy, whistling, clapping, and cheering.

"Bro," Logan said, scooping the puck out of the net and sliding it down the ice to the waiting kids, "that was pretty neat. Nice shot."

"Thanks, mate," Preston replied, doing a small bow, "I didn't know if I could pull it off."

Millie was next in line, taking a puck and slowly skating up the ice toward Khloe, who was waiting in the net. As she moved up the ice, she dropped it between her skates and then kicked it back up onto her stick and decided it was now or never, doing a series of twirls like a figure skater before launching a wrist shot up and over Khloe, who'd dropped down low.

The goal got a big round of applause, and even Khloe was laughing.

"You look dizzy, Mills," Khloe said laughing, "from all those crazy twirls."

"I'm not going to lie," Millie replied, "I almost fell over. I'm not sure how the puck managed to go in at all. It's lucky I didn't just fall over and slide into the net myself!"

For the kids, this was much more than just another game. For some of them, it could be the last time they played hockey together and, even more importantly, the last time they would play hockey against one another.

"Okay, kids, let's wrap it up and head to the benches," Coach Phil said, calling out to all the kids, "and parents, make sure you're sitting close to the benches so I don't have to shout." Once all the kids were gathered together, Coach Phil was ready to speak.

"Coach John and I would like to thank you for coming today for one last game and also congratulate you on your graduation. I hope you all enjoyed the surprise. We also want to thank you for your hard work over the last few years. And generally, for being such a dedicated and hardworking group. Remember, whatever life throws at you or whatever direction you take, remember all the good times we had together. These memories we made will last you a lifetime, and if things get hard, you can look back at them and remember that there are always good times. Jeez, I'm starting to get a little bit emotional, Coach John. Do you want to take over?"

"Of course," Coach John began, "Coach Phil is right. You've been an awesome group of kids, and it has been a pleasure to coach you all over the years. Who knows, maybe in four years, we'll all be back here celebrating you graduating from high school. When we started coaching you all, we never expected to get more than a team of kids to coach. What we ended up with is a family. But enough from me before I start tearing up, too. Coach Phil will announce the prizes for tonight."

"Yes, the prizes. Can't forget those. First, the award for best trick shot goes to Millie. That foot drag and kick up into the twirl and actually managing to score a goal was impressive," Coach Phil said, handing over a small trophy and envelope, "well done."

"Thanks, Coach," Millie replied, taking a bow before opening the envelope and finding a $100 Sports World voucher. "Wow, thanks guys!"

"You're welcome. Next up is Hunter. While your shot wasn't as tricky as Millie's, the speed skating and power behind that shot was super impressive."

"Thanks, Coach," Hunter replied, accepting his trophy and envelope before sitting back down.

"And finally, for the goalie who let in the least number of goals," Coach Phil said, drawing it out a little for the crowd, "Khloe takes the prize, letting in one less goal than Logan. Bad luck, Logan, but well done, Khloe!"

"Way to go, Khloe!" Logan shouted and clapped.

"Thanks, Coach," Khloe said, taking her prizes, "it's not easy being as good as me, but if y'all work hard, you too could be an amazing goalie."

"Okay, thanks again, kids. It's been amazing. Now, for one last thing. Photos have been requested by the parents, so we'll have you all line up in your teams. No complaining. Go and look your best! Once we get off the ice, we have a pizza party waiting upstairs!"

The kids lined up for what felt like thousands of photos together, team photos, individual photos, and just about every pose imaginable. Then, it was upstairs for a pizza party and a final chance to hang out before heading home for the evening.

14

"WELL," MILLIE'S MOM said as they all walked into the house, "that was an emotional roller-coaster I wasn't expecting."

"I know, right?" Millie agreed, "laughing, crying, laughing. I couldn't keep up."

"Run upstairs, grab a shower, and when you're done, we'll give you your graduation present."

"Ooh," Millie answered, "sounds good. I'll be right back."

It was possibly the fastest shower that Millie had ever taken, and she was back downstairs within ten minutes, ready to see what her parents had gotten her as a graduation gift.

"First," her dad began, "we want to say congratulations. With everything you've gone through at school and hockey and how much harder you need

SAM LAWRENCE & BEN JACKSON

to work, you did an outstanding job, and this present is just our way of saying that we noticed and we appreciate it."

"Thanks, guys," Millie said, reaching out to take the envelope her dad held in his hand, quickly tearing it open.

As she tore the end off the envelope, a ticket tumbled out onto the floor. Bending down to pick it up, Millie immediately recognized that it was a plane ticket.

"Guys! Are we going on a holiday?" Millie shouted before looking down at the tickets and reading the names and destinations. "Wait, this one is for me, and it's to Las Vegas? Mia lives in Las Vegas. Can we see her while we're there?"

"We're not going to Las Vegas," her mom explained, "you're going to Las Vegas. And Georgia is going with you."

"Guys!" Millie shouted, jumping up and down, "Are you both messing with me? This isn't a prank, is it? Wait, you're letting us fly to Las Vegas on the plane alone?"

"We're not that crazy," Millie's mom replies, "Mia's dad is going to be in town for a training exercise, and he's going to fly back to Las Vegas with you both. A couple of days before the end of your holiday, your father and I will fly down for a couple of days to do some sightseeing and shopping, and we'll all fly home together."

"This is so cool," Millie replied, hugging both her parents, "wait. Does Georgia already know? What about Mia? When are their parents telling them?"

"I texted Mia and Georgia's moms while you were taking a shower. They're all finding out at the same time you are," her mom answered, just as Millie's phone started beeping with multiple message notifications. "Judging by the sound of your phone, they both just found out. Go ahead, answer them."

Millie picked up the video phone call from Georgia and instantly started screaming. Moments later, Mia came on the call, and now all three of them were screaming and trying to talk at a million miles an hour.

"Enough," Millie's dad shouted, "take it upstairs, you three. I don't think my eardrums can take the squealing and giggling anymore.

"Thanks, Mom," Millie said, hugging her mom, "and thanks, Dad. It really is the best surprise ever."

"You're welcome, honey," her mom replied, "now go and make some plans with your friends, and this time, you can make them for real," she said with a wink.

"So," Millie began, "we have an entire week in Las Vegas with you, Mia. What are we going to be doing?"

"How cool was it of our parents to plan this whole thing without letting any of us get the slightest clue?" Mia said, "I had no idea they were planning anything. I thought I'd just get a gift voucher or something."

"I know, right?" Millie replied, "they really hit this one out of the park. Not sure how they plan on topping it, though."

"Right," Georgia agreed, "they really went above and beyond."

"Big win for the parents on this gift," Millie said laughing, "but getting back to planning the trip. Is there anything specific anyone wants to do?"

"I want to go shopping for sure," Georgia added before Mia even had a chance to suggest anything, "so can we have one day where we all go and get manicures, pedicures, and maybe a spa day?"

"Sure," Mia said laughing. "That sounds great. One day for beauty treatments."

"Do you think we can visit the Grand Canyon and the Hoover Dam?" Millie asked, "will your mom be able to drive us?"

"Let me go and ask," Mia said, running out of her room and returning a few minutes later, "she said that's fine. She's going to book off work for a couple of days, so we can plan to do any of the longer driving things on those days. What else do you guys want to do?"

The three girls brainstormed a bunch of different ideas while Mia wrote them all down, and they started to sketch together a rough schedule for their vacation.

Three weeks had gone by, with Millie, Cameron, and their families enjoying their traditional summer vacation at the cottage. However, this vacation was a little different than all the rest.

Firstly, not only did Cameron and Millie have to get used to being boyfriend and girlfriend, but so did their parents. Seeing the two teenagers walking around, holding hands, and hugging one another took a little bit of getting used to, but it was nothing the parents couldn't handle.

Now that they were back, the group of friends could finally get together and had planned a trip to the amusement park to take advantage of their season passes.

A shuttle bus would pick them all up from town, which meant their parents wouldn't have to drive them and pick them up, then drop them back at the city at the end of the day.

They had an hour or so on the bus, and everyone was interested in grilling Cameron and Millie about their holiday.

"So," Daylyn asked Millie and Cameron, "was the '*family*' vacation a little awkward this year?"

"Yeah," Khloe asked, "how were all the parents seeing you two as boyfriend and girlfriend?"

"They were fine," Cameron replied, "after the first day or so anyway."

"Yeah, the first day was a little strange," Millie agreed, "but then they were fine. I think because they already knew about us before, it made the whole thing a lot easier."

Once they arrived at the park, the group of kids went straight for the Big Dropper, one of the tallest amusement rides in the world. It was a straight drop-down, but instead of going straight up and down like a lot of other drop rides, it started spinning one way on the way up and then spun the opposite way on the way down.

There were a few green and white faces after that first ride, but they all agreed to do it again before they left for the day and moved on to some of the other rides.

Because they'd all got the season passes with fast pass, it also meant that they could skip the lines and had priority at many of the different stores and amusements throughout the entire park.

SAM LAWRENCE & BEN JACKSON

For the rest of the day, the group of friends forgot about middle school ending and high school starting and instead had fun together, riding the rides, eating junk food, and just laughing and enjoying their time together.

15

THE SUMMER HAD been one to remember, with the kids from Dakota enjoying their break before they transitioned from middle school to high school. Rather than dwell on the sadness of who would be going to school with whom and where, they'd instead focused on just having fun together and taking advantage of the beautiful warm weather.

As the final days of the summer break drew inevitably closer, the Dakota crew arranged one last night together, with a firepit, movie, and BBQ at Cameron's house. Once everyone had arrived and found somewhere to sit, the conversation switched to Millie and Georgia's trip to Las Vegas to catch up with Mia.

"So, was Las Vegas cool?" Khloe asked, "I've never been, but it looks pretty cool."

"It was hot," Georgia said. "Every time we left the house, I felt as if my face was melting off."

"Yeah, last year when I went with my parents, it was crazy hot." Preston added, "it's not on my top ten places to live, that's for sure."

"Yeah. I think that's why hockey is so popular. It gives you the chance to get out of the heat for a little bit and into the arena where it's nice and cold," Millie said laughing.

"Oh, how was the hockey scene there?" Rhys asked, "Do they have many teams, and are they any good?"

"We went to a game and borrowed some equipment to have a quick game during one of Mia's practices. She's definitely the best player on her team, but the rest aren't too bad," Georgia answered, "not at my level, of course, but let's be honest, who is?"

It wasn't long before the conversation switched to what everyone would be doing after the school holidays finished and they went off to high school. While most of the kids would still be going to the same high school as everyone else, there were a few who would be pursuing a different education path.

"Sage," Rhys said quietly, "tell everyone your news."

"Oh, yeah. I got accepted into Trinity School of Arts," Sage said proudly, but not without a hint of sadness creeping into her voice.

Everyone congratulated her. Trinity was a fantastic school that was extremely hard to get into. Very few kids got accepted, but it was still only thirty minutes out of town, so they'd be able to catch up regularly, and it wouldn't impact her hockey schedule too much at all.

"I guess it's time to give everyone my news," Preston said, "I got accepted into Banks STEM Academy."

This news was the most shocking to the group. They all knew that the Banks STEM Academy was in the next state over because all their STEM courses used information from that school.

"Oh, that's so far away," Georgia said, looking from Ashlyn to Preston, "but what about you two?"

"We decided that it would be easier if we just stayed friends. The school is so far away, and I'll most likely only be home on weekends. We've both known for a few weeks now, but I didn't want to ruin everyone's holidays, so I kept it a secret," Preston explained, still holding hands with Ashlyn.

Ashlyn had known since Preston found out and had only told her sister Daylyn when she'd found her crying about the news. The Banks STEM Academy had approached Preston about applying during a robotics event he'd won.

"Congratulations, buddy. You work so hard with your robotics stuff. You deserve it. I guess since everyone's sharing—" Cameron began to say before being interrupted by Rhys.

"You're not going anywhere!" he shouted, "Don't even think about it."

"I know," Cameron replied, rolling his eyes, "I was going to tell everyone about my business. I've been doing odd jobs, mowing lawns, washing windows and cars, and cleaning out yards. So far, I've managed to save almost $500 towards my car fund. In the winter, I will switch to shoveling snow, and I applied to be a referee at the arena for the house league and junior games."

"That's great, Cam," Ashlyn said, "you always were a hard worker. Are you going to be a ref, too, Mills? You'd be good at it."

"I wanted to," Millie replied, "and I applied, but one of Mom's friends has a shop in the mall, and she asked Mom if I would be interested in working after school, so I think I'm going to do that."

"That's right near me," Khloe explained, "remember the fundraiser we did at the Italian restaurant? With Mr. Rossi? I applied for a kitchen hand or dishwasher job, and he said yes. I'm going to be working in the kitchen Thursday, Friday, and Saturday nights once school starts."

"That's awesome, Khloe," Logan said, "I think I'll have to start dropping in for some Italian food!"

"Has anyone met with the high school counselor yet?" Millie asked, "I went in yesterday and went through all of my courses and workload for next year."

"Who is this, and what have you done with my disorganized friend?" Georgia said with a wink.

"Funny, but I'm actually excited about high school. It's going to be a lot different than middle school, and I'll need to get into my routine and schedule again. Kind of excited and nervous at the same time."

"You'll be fine, Millie," Preston said, "you did so much better last year. We all noticed how much more relaxed you were."

"Plus, you started to show up to things on time," Rhys added with a smirk, "instead of running into the arena dropping skates and equipment all over the place."

"Or showing up to school still eating your breakfast," Cameron said, chiming in, "with half your hair brushed."

"Hey!" Millie said, punching him on the arm, "whose side are you on anyway? Besides, you love messy hair and tracksuit pants."

"I must do," Cameron said, squeezing her hand and smiling back at her.

After everyone had said their goodbyes, it was just Millie and Cameron left, watching the firepit burn itself out as the stars slowly made their journey across the sky.

"I'm excited, nervous, and sad all at the same time," Millie said quietly.

"Same," Cameron said, "but we'll have each other."

"No matter what, promise me we'll always be friends."

"Of course," Cameron said, feeling Millie squeeze his hand, "no matter what."

"Thank you," Millie replied, resting her head on his shoulders.

The two best friends sat that way for the next hour, slowly watching the stars and listening to the crackling of the fire.

It had been quite an adventure for the group of friends from Dakota, and as they headed into high school and all the challenges that would come with it, their journey was only just beginning.

The End. Or is it?

Made in the USA
Monee, IL
30 October 2024

d25577aa-7e94-43e2-b3d6-5fa36dadea1eR01